ANNIE ROSE
IS MY
LITTLE SISTER

For Jack

ANNIE ROSE IS MY LITTLE SISTER
A RED FOX BOOK 9781 782 95616 7

First published in Great Britain by The Bodley Head,
an imprint of Random House Children's Publishers UK
A Penguin Random House Company

Penguin
Random House
UK

The Bodley Head edition published 2002
Red Fox edition published 2003
This Red Fox edition published 2015

1 3 5 7 9 10 8 6 4 2

Copyright © Shirley Hughes, 2002

Red Fox Books are published by Random House Children's Publishers UK,
61–63 Uxbridge Road, London W5 5SA

www.**randomhousechildrens**.co.uk
www.**randomhouse**.co.uk

Addresses for companies within The Random House Group Limited can be found at:
www.randomhouse.co.uk/offices.htm

THE RANDOM HOUSE GROUP Limited Reg. No. 954009

A CIP catalogue record for this book is available from the British Library.

Printed in China

Penguin Random House is committed to a sustainable future for our business, our readers
and our planet. This book is made from Forest Stewardship Council® certified paper.

ANNIE ROSE
IS MY
LITTLE SISTER

Shirley Hughes

RED FOX

Annie Rose is my little sister. She likes books a lot and she's always wanting me to look at them with her.

She's quite good at playing games.
She likes it when I hide under a sheet
and pop out at her – Boo!

But when I'm really
hiding she can hardly
ever find me.

One of Annie Rose's favourite toys
is her little chest of drawers. She likes
opening and shutting each one.

She puts all sorts of things inside them. Sometimes she pulls out all the drawers and makes them into beds for her family of mice.

The only things I have in my bed when I go to sleep are my bit of blanket and my elephant, Flumbo. He is quite old, nearly as old as me. But Annie Rose has lots of things in her cot.

Early in the morning I can hear her throwing them out on to the floor, one by one – thump, thump, thump! Then the only thing she has left in there is Buttercup, her lamb. She doesn't often throw her out.

Annie Rose always wants to play with my toys. She seems to like them better than her own, which is very annoying.

When I want to lay out all my cars and trucks and rail track I have to do it on the table where she can't get at them.

Our best game, which we play together, is shops. When we have a shop indoors we set out all the little packets and boxes and plastic bottles with screw tops which Mum has saved for us, and we arrange all sorts of nice things on plates from Annie Rose's tea set.

Then I am the shopkeeper, Mr Lewis Burrows, and Annie Rose is my helper.

Sometimes Annie Rose wants to make her own shop in the back garden. She has leaf plates and sells empty snail shells and daisy heads.

But she can't make a daisy chain.
Neither can I.
   Only Mum can do that.

When we go to the seaside Dad and I
make a huge sandcastle with turrets and
tunnels and a moat all around which fills
up with water when the tide comes in.
Annie Rose can only make sand pies.
But they are very good ones.

Annie Rose doesn't like the sea much.
She prefers kicking up the water in
shallow pools.

But Dad and I like diving into big,
rough waves.

Annie Rose can be really awful
sometimes. She gets into a rage and
lies on the floor and screams and
kicks. It is most awful when she does
this in a shop.

She usually cheers up again, after a
while.

Annie Rose's best friends are Marian and Lily. They play together a lot. Sometimes – not very often – Marian and Lily only want to play with each other and they don't want Annie Rose. And that makes her very sad.

My best friend is Bernard. When he comes to play at our house Annie Rose always wants to join in. She laughs and laughs when Bernard pretends to be a prehistoric monster, showing its fierce teeth and making terrible noises.

Annie Rose loves Bernard.

But when Annie Rose cries, or wakes up from her nap in a cross mood, I'm the only person who can cheer her up.

Because she's my little
sister, and I'm her brother,

and we'll go on being that for ever . . .

. . . even until we're grown up.